FAERIEGROUND

Return to the Crows

Book Eleven

BY BETH BRACKEN AND KAY FRASER
ILLUSTRATED BY ODESSA SAWYER

STONE ARCH BOOKS
a capstone imprint

FAERIEGROUND IS PUBLISHED BY
STONE ARCH BOOKS
A CAPSTONE IMPRINT
1710 ROE CREST DRIVE
NORTH MANKATO, MINNESOTA 56003
WWW.CAPSTONEPUB.COM

LIBRARY OF CONGRESS CATALOGING-IN-PUBLICATION DATA

BRACKEN, BETH, AUTHOR.

  RETURN TO THE CROWS / BY BETH BRACKEN AND KAY FRASER ;
ILLUSTRATED BY ODESSA SAWYER.

    PAGES CM. -- (FAERIEGROUND ; 11)

  SUMMARY: AS LUCY, KHEELAN, AND THE UNITED FAERIE MARCH
TO WAR AGAINST THE CROWS, SOLI DISCOVERS WHO HAS BEEN
SMUGGLING KHEELAN'S MESSAGES TO HER, AND LEARNS CARO'S
SECRET--AND LUCY'S MOTHER RETURNS TO THE FAERIEGROUND.

  ISBN 978-1-4342-9187-5 (LIBRARY BINDING) -- ISBN 978-1-4342-
9191-2 (PBK.)

1. FAIRIES--JUVENILE FICTION. 2. BEST FRIENDS--JUVENILE
FICTION. 3. MAGIC--JUVENILE FICTION. 4. RESCUES--JUVENILE
FICTION. 5. MOTHERS AND DAUGHTERS--JUVENILE FICTION. [1.
FAIRIES--FICTION. 2. BEST FRIENDS--FICTION. 3. FRIENDSHIP--
FICTION. 4. MAGIC--FICTION. 5. RESCUES--FICTION. 6. SECRETS-
-FICTION. 7. MOTHERS AND DAUGHTERS--FICTION.] I. FRASER,
KAY, AUTHOR. II. SAWYER, ODESSA, ILLUSTRATOR. III. TITLE. IV.
SERIES: BRACKEN, BETH. FAERIEGROUND ; [BK. 11]

  PZ7.B6989RE 2014

  813.6--DC23

                                      2014002994

BOOK DESIGN BY K. FRASER

ALL PHOTOS © SHUTTERSTOCK WITH THESE EXCEPTIONS:
AUTHOR PORTRAIT © K FRASER AND ILLUSTRATOR PORTRAIT
© ODESSA SAWYER

PRINTED IN CANADA.
032014
008086FRF14

"Those who don't believe in magic
will never find it."
– Roald Dahl

For Etta, my daughter. — BB
To the love of my life and best friend, JB — KF

The newborn princess was adored
by her mother.

But her mother couldn't stay. Her mother had to leave, as much as she loved the baby. And so the baby was raised by her father.

It would be nice to say he tried his best, but it wouldn't be true.

Chapter 1

Lucy

We have spent two days preparing.

The morning that we're supposed to leave is cold and wet. Hundreds of faeries—and I—gather near the palace where Calandra used to live. Jonn is barking orders. The other leaders—Lotham, Helenea, Motherbird, Montan, and Calla—are already on their horses, yelling to their own groups.

Kheelan stands near me, holding his horse's reins and scribbling something on a ragged piece of paper. He folds the piece of paper and lets out an ear-splitting whistle. A large black bird swoops down out of nowhere.

Kheelan tucks the paper into a thin band that's tied around the bird's neck. Then Kheelan whispers something, and the bird flies away.

"It is time," Jonn calls. "We ride for Roseland. And we ride for all of the faerie kingdoms."

Everyone cheers. But then the other leaders ride up next to him. The area becomes silent.

"We know that some of us will die," Montan says, his indigo cloak smooth behind him. "The Crows will show no restraint. They expect us."

Then Motherbird, wearing a red dress, rides forward, and they are still again. She looks out over the group, and then up at the sky. "The Crows gather," she says. "We must ride."

With that, the faeries begin to move. I climb onto my horse, and as if she knows exactly what to do, she begins to trot forward.

Motherbird rides up next to me. "Your mother will cross over," she says.

"I know," I tell her.

"She is dangerous here," Motherbird says. Her face is kind. "But she is still your mother, and she still loves you."

I take a deep breath. "Okay," I say. "I'll try to remember that."

"You'll need to," she says.

We continue to ride, the horses moving faster.

Motherbird points to my chest. "You wear the Crows' color," she says. The necklace, she means.

"Keep it safe, and it will keep you safe," she says. "But do not let anyone take it from you. No one. If it falls into the wrong hands, it will devastate us. All of us."

"Okay," I say. "Do you want to take it?"

She smiles. "Heavens, no," she says. "I won't live through this. But you will. You are the person who can protect it. You are the Light One, and you are here to help us fight against the dark. Be careful, Lucy. But be brave."

Chapter 2

Soli

If I want to get a message to Kheelan before they come for me, I need to find out who's helping him get messages to me.

So after our morning classes, I hide. I hide under my bed and wait, just me and the cobwebs and the dust bunnies.

There's a knock, and I stiffen.

The door swings open. I recognize Caro's boots. "Soli?" she says.

I don't say anything, of course. I stay under the bed, silent as I can be. She walks closer, and I hear the creak of the window being opened.

The sound of beating wings enters the room.

"Good bird," Caro says.

I hear the wings again, leaving, and then she closes the window. Paper rustles, and then she walks back to the door.

But she doesn't leave. "I know you're here," she says, her voice low and calm. "Don't make me look under the bed, Soli."

I sigh. Then I crawl out. She doesn't bother trying to explain. She just reaches out and hands me a folded piece of paper. "I think we have a problem," she says.

"You read it?" I ask, but I know it doesn't

matter.

Sweet—

It is dawn, and we are flying toward you.

yours—

K.

I look at Caro. "So it was you the whole time,"

I say.

"Yes," she says. A smile twists on her face.

"Didn't you know? It's in my name. Caro, the

Betrayer."

Chapter 3

Soli

"I'm sorry I read your letters,"
Caro says.

We are in her greenhouse tower room,

watching out the window for approaching

faeries.

I shrug. "It's okay," I say. And it is. At first I felt

embarrassed, but I have nothing to be ashamed

of. I haven't done anything wrong.

"Are you going to tell my father?" she asks

quietly. "I know he would listen to you. He'd

be furious with me, but he'd believe you."

"Of course not," I say. "Why would I tell him?

It would get me in trouble too."

"Because it could get me out of the way,"

she says. "If you told him, he'd banish me or

something. And you could be the princess

here, and eventually the queen."

"I don't want to be the princess here," I say. I

look around the room. "I mean, it's beautiful

and everything. And most people have been

kind to me since I decided to stay. But——"

"But the Crows are terrible," she says.

We stare at each other.

"You think I'm terrible too," she says.

I sigh. "Caro, I don't know what to think about you," I say, and it's true.

Caro, the Betrayer. So far, she's betrayed everyone, over and over again. I don't understand her. But I do like her.

"I understand," she says, her face looking hurt.

"I don't think you do," I say. "You've betrayed everyone. But I do like you. And I do believe that you weren't trying to get me in trouble."

She looks up at me. "Why would you get in trouble? You weren't the one betraying the Crows. You've probably never done anything wrong in your life." Then a twinkle glints in her eye. "Yet," she says.

I smile. "Yet," I say.

We watch out the window for a while longer. "When they come, whose side are you on?" I ask finally.

Caro shrugs. "I'm on my own side, like always," she says.

I don't know what that means. Is her side my side? Or is her side whichever side doesn't get her killed?

She can tell that's what I'm trying to understand. "I'm on the side of winning," she says. "But I don't know who will win this."

We stare out at the lush forest past the valley.

"I wonder what my mother would have done, if she were here," I say. "I mean, as the queen. Not my other human mother. The faerie one."

"I don't remember my mother," Caro says. "It must be interesting to have two."

"I don't know much about Calandra," I admit. "What happened to your mother?"

She is silent, and I feel bad. I shouldn't have asked something so personal.

"She ran away," she says finally. "She ran back to the humans."

She looks me in the eye and adds, "My mother is Andria."

Chapter 4

Soli

Caro tells me.

Three years before Calandra gave birth to me, her older sister, Andria, came to the faerieground.

She had been obsessed with faeries for years—she knew they could be reached through Willow Forest, outside Mearston. She wanted, more than anything, to cross over and meet them. She wanted to become one.

She finally crossed over, with help from the Mearston Historical Society. And when she did, the first person she met was the young Crow prince, Georg.

They fell in love, even though Andria was human and Georg was a faerie. They were married. And then Georg's father died, and Georg became king, and Andria became queen.

Caro was born a little more than a year after Andria came to the faeries. And a few months after that, Calandra came to save her sister. Andria was sent home, and Calandra stayed. A year later, I was born.

Caro never knew she had a half-sister until Lucy arrived in the faerieground.

Looking at Caro now, I can't believe I didn't notice it before. She and Lucy have the same coloring, the same quick grin, the same mischievous eyes.

"So you're my cousin," I say. "Our mothers were sisters."

She nods. "Yes," she says. "And I'm sorry for— for everything I've done to you."

"I forgive you," I say finally. Then I ask, "So you don't remember Andria at all?"

Caro shakes her head. "No. What is she like?"

I think about Andria. "She was like a mother to me," I say. "A second mother." Then I laugh. "A third mother, I guess. She was kind. She protected me. I always believed that she loved me."

"I wonder if she loves me," Caro whispers. A tear slips from her eye, but before I can say anything to try to make her feel better, she leaps up and crosses the room. "I want to give you something," she says. "My mother's journal." She pulls a book from under a bench.

"From when she was here?" I ask.

Caro nods. "She wrote in it every day. Maybe you'd like to read it."

"What's it like?" I ask.

She shrugs. "I haven't read it," she admits. "Honestly, I've been so mad at her for leaving. And I don't really like reading anyway."

"I'd love to look at it," I say. "Thank you."

She hands me the book. And then we sit, and watch, and wait.

Chapter 5

Lucy

We ride all day.

By nightfall, I'm starting to have a hard time feeling my legs. Kheelan rides effortlessly. I envy his confidence, his skills. He catches me staring. I feel myself blush and look away.

I think about how Kheelan and I met—locked together in a cell. "Remember when we met?" I ask. "Why were you in the cell?"

He laughs. "My father was mad at me," he says. "Wanted to teach me a lesson, I suppose."

"Why was he mad?"

He shrugs. "I was always disobeying him," he explains. "Trying to get over to the human world, trying to explore the faerieground, going out of the boundaries of Roseland."

"And he wasn't okay with that?" I ask, surprised. Jonn seems like an adventurer.

"He was Queen Calandra's personal guard," Kheelan says with a smile. "I was an embarrassment to him. So once in a while, he'd throw me in the cells." He looks up at his father, riding far in front of us. "I guess things have changed," he adds quietly.

I think we must be far beyond the boundaries of Roseland. "Where are we?" I ask.

"Crow land," Kheelan says.

"It gives me the creeps," I tell him.

"Try to take your mind off it," he says. "Tell me how you first came to the faerieground."

"Don't you know?" I ask, and he shakes his head. "Soli sent me here, by mistake."

He laughs. "How did she do that?"

"She made a wish in the woods," I say quietly. "It seems like so long ago, but really, it was only a few weeks. How weird."

"What was her wish?"

I sigh. Then I tell him the whole story.

"You kissed the boy she loved," he says.

"Not loved," I say, laughing. "She just thought he was nice. He made her feel important."

"Why did you kiss him?" he asks.

I shrug. "I guess he made me feel important too," I say quietly.

Kheelan smiles. "Everyone makes mistakes," he says. "And I have to admit, I'm not sorry. I do believe Soli would have crossed over someday no matter what, but I'm glad I met her then."

"I'm glad too," I say.

"I hope we aren't too late to save her," he says. "I hope—" But he stops. Then he straightens his shoulders and rides ahead quickly, leaving me alone.

Chapter 6

Andria

Day 4

The faeries are not what I expected. They're darker. Meaner. More interesting. I want to be one of them. I want to be more than human. I want to belong here.

There must be a way to become faerie. I can't really ask anyone, but I've hinted at it, and so far no one seems to know anything.

Georg knows my secret wish, though. He asked me to take a walk in the woods with him tomorrow night, and I'm going to. He said he might have information that could help me. So far he's the only one who wants to help me.

Daily, he finds me, to sit and talk and laugh for a while, so I don't feel too alone. He knows I don't want to go home, not ever.

Is it crazy to think that Georg and I might have a future together? Is it crazy to hope for that?

I don't know if I'll be able to sleep tonight, knowing that we have plans for tomorrow.

Is it a date? Maybe I can think of it like that, secretly. Just for myself. A date with a prince in the faerieground woods.

Chapter 7

Soli

The first things that catch my eye are the banners of color coming toward the castle.

Caro is asleep next to me on the bench, and I shake her awake. "Look," I say. "They're coming."

She gazes out the window. Dawn has broken and it looks like most of the faerieground is headed fast into the Crows' valley.

"How long before they're here?" I ask.

She shrugs. "Maybe fifteen minutes."

"How long before your father knows they're here?"

She narrows her eyes at me and laughs. "Don't be stupid," she says, that familiar meanness creeping back into her voice. "He knew they were coming before we did. He probably knew they were coming before they did."

"What should we do?" I ask, stumbling to my feet.

She slowly stands. "Let's go downstairs," she says. "I don't want them to come for us."

"Who?" I ask, and she gives me that look again.

"The army," she tells me. "Come on."

In the throne room, Georg looks out the window at the valley. He looks fearless, strong, frightening.

Then Georg turns to me. "I believe I have you to thank for this turn of events," he says, but he doesn't look angry. He looks hungry. "It's been years in the making, but finally, they've found a reason strong enough to threaten us."

My stomach turns with fear.

"You'll both fight on the front lines," he says, walking toward the door. Then he stops, turns back to me. "Once they see you're on our side," he says, "they will know there's no hope. They will surrender to me, and the Crows will finally rule the faerieground, the way we ought to."

I don't say anything. I have to pretend to go along with this. "I have one request, sir," I say, bowing my head. "I would like to wear my crown. If they see me as their queen turned against them, rather than a simple girl, I think they'll be more likely to give up. Don't you?"

A spark flashes in the king's eyes. "Brilliant," he says. "I'll have your crown returned to your room while you dress."

I bow and follow Caro before I can say anything else.

I don't know where this idea came from, but I think I need my crown. Of course King Georg knows its power, but he doesn't think I know, and he thinks I'm a Crow now. He thinks I'd never do anything to fight against him. He thinks I'm stupid. He thinks I'd fight my own people. He thinks wrong.

Chapter 8

Lucy

It starts before we reach
the clearing.

Huge, black birds swoop down toward us, darkening the sky. The first line of horses rushes into the valley anyway.

"Charge!" Jonn screams. "Bows to the sky. Get those birds on the ground!" Everyone follows his command.

The yelling of all the faeries grows louder. Horses stumble and fall to the ground as the birds attack their riders. Birds sink from the sky, but I'm sure there are far more of them than there are of us.

This isn't what I expected. It's much worse.

I pull on the reins, bringing my horse to a halt, at the same moment that a bird soars straight into Kheelan's horse's face, poking at its eyes.

Kheelan leaps off, pointing an arrow straight at the bird's heart. He lets it go and the bird falls, but the horse has already been blinded.

I ride closer. "Are you okay?" I ask. There's so much fear in my voice, I'm embarrassed. "Get on my horse," I add.

He shakes his head. "They are looking for me," he yells. "Get away, Lucy! You're not safe near me." He looks up at me, shading his eyes. "Find Motherbird. And Lucy, put your necklace away!"

I look down. The necklace has found its way out of my shirt, so I quickly tuck it in. Then I turn my horse around and head toward the back of the group, looking for Motherbird and the other Ladybirds.

Finally, I see the flush of red bringing up the rear of our army.

As I ride closer, I can see that the Ladybirds'
arrows shoot red smoke toward the sky. I see a
brush of red riding down the clearing.

A hand grabs my arm, and I turn. It's
Motherbird. "Follow me," she says.

My horse turns in her direction, following her
without me guiding it. Just as we enter the
castle grounds, Motherbird pulls me behind a
boulder in a garden filled with black-petaled
tulips.

"Are you afraid?" she asks.

I shake my head, although we both know that's a lie. "Is my mother here already?" I ask.

She shakes her head, but I believe her.

She pulls her own pendant out from beneath her cloak. It's the same as the one I wear, except that it's a deep, ruby red.

"When the kingdom was split, we were each given a key," she says. "All seven keys can make the kingdom whole again. But the necklaces must be whole—they must all be safe."

I frown. "If we have all seven, can't we just put them together?"

"No," she says. "The necklaces are bound to their owners—the rulers of the seven kingdoms. Georg must agree."

"I understand," I say.

"Good," she says. "Now we must return to the fight. And you must stay safe, so please, Lucy, stay behind me. I know what to expect, but fate can always change."

The Crow army is pouring out of the castle. I pull my horse behind Motherbird's and follow her forward.

Yelling—and the piercing whistles of speedy arrows—comes from the two armies as they meet on the grounds before us. The warriors are dressed in black, with black metal armor and black metal helmets. They are far more protected than the army from the other kingdoms. And on the front line, right in the middle of the group, I see a helmetless girl, in a crown, with the face of my best friend.

Chapter 9

Andria

Day 426

I promised to keep it a secret, but I can't. I told the one person who can't tell anyone in the kingdom. I'm too happy to keep it to myself. I had to tell her, even though I know she won't understand.

I miss Calandra, I do—I think of her often. It's true that we haven't always seen eye to eye. The opposite, really. But she's my sister, my lifelong best friend.

My lifelong worst enemy, sometimes. But my sister, all the same.

I've known her for nineteen years, since my mother first held her out to me.

When we were small, I never kept a secret from Calandra, and she never kept a secret from me. Our lives were open books. We shared everything. After all, I'm only a year older than she is—we really grew up together, spent all our time together.

Of course, all that changed when I learned about the faeries.

How could she think this place didn't exist?

And worse, how could she think it would be a place full of sadness, or badness, or anything other than a perfect place full of happiness?

Perhaps, as the new queen, I am biased. Maybe after a hundred years here I will see some dark side to the faerieground. Perhaps I won't always feel like I stumbled into paradise.

I almost wish I could bring Calandra here to tell her, to show her. Faced with the beauties of this place, she would have to understand. She would have to see what I have always seen.

And, like I said, I do miss her.

So I had to send my sister a message.

I had to tell her she was going to be an aunt.

I had to tell her that a half-faerie child is growing inside me.

And if Georg and I find the right spell before she's born, the baby I carry will be all faerie— and so will I.

Chapter 10

Soli

My crown is heavy on my head as
I face the faerie army.

"Don't hurt anyone," I whisper to Caro.

She narrows her eyes. "I'll try," she says. "Don't worry about hitting a bird," she adds. "They're all ours."

Then we fight. Caro and I work well together, and we're sneaky. Together, we disarm other Crows. We take down the circling birds. We never once hit someone from the other army.

The rainbow of soldiers spreads out before us. The Crows aren't letting them get any closer to the castle.

But as we fight, I start to see that the other faeries recognize me. They truly do think I'm fighting against them.

I start to feel afraid. And then a shower of arrows comes our way.

In a flash, Mikael dives toward us, knocking us to the ground. The arrows miss, but only by a millimeter. They hit Mikael instead. He grunts in pain, but stands up anyway.

"Are you okay?" I ask, but he pushes me aside and walks away.

My crown has fallen off, so I put it in my backpack and put my Crow helmet on my head.

Then I hear my name. "Soli!" cries the familiar voice. It's Kheelan. But I don't see him.

Then there's a break in the crowd, and he rushes toward me on foot. He sees me. He stops. In the middle of the war, he stares at me.

Then he points his bow in my direction, and the arrow flies toward me.

Chapter 11

Andria

Day 793

Calandra is here. I can't believe it. My sister, here. I can't believe she was able to cross over. It took me years to figure it out, and she comes just months after receiving my message that Caro was born?

When she met Georg today, she seemed horrified. Like he was some kind of monster. You'd think she'd be excited to meet her sister's husband, the father of her sister's new baby.

She held Caro, but didn't seem to love her.

If only the spells had worked. If only I was a pure faerie now, instead of the human queen. Then she'd see. She'd see how much I've changed, being here. She'd see what a wonderful place it is.

I can't believe it. She doesn't even understand how much I love Georg.

She went straight up to him in the throne room and told him to release me. That it isn't safe here for me and that I need to go home where I belong.

I laughed then. Home? Where I belong? I belong here. This is my home.

Georg laughed too, of course. He knows I belong here. He knows I love it here. And he told her that. He told her that he could have chosen any faerie girl to marry, but he chose me. And that I chose him. And that our daughter—beautiful, sweet Caro—is proof of our love.

He found Calandra a room to sleep in, even though I said we should send her back. He said he wanted her to be comfortable.

Tonight, he told me his plan. He thinks she will not go without trying to save me. And so we can use her presence here to put a grand scheme into place. Something he has wanted for years.

To bring the faerieground together, with him as the king. I told him I'll do anything I need to do to make the plan work.

And then he told me what I will have to do. What my part of the plan will be. I will have to leave. And it may be years before I can come back.

Chapter 12

Soli

Kheelan's eyes don't leave mine as his arrow grazes my hair, landing behind me.

I hear the thud of a Crow's body hitting the ground. I let out a long breath. He wasn't aiming at me. He trusts me. He knows I'm still me. He knows I'm not one of them.

I drop my bow and run to him. He kisses me, wraps his arms around me. "You're here," I say.

"You're safe," he says. We cling together in the middle of the chaos.

I know I'm supposed to pretend to be on the Crow side, but I can't. Not now. Not with Kheelan standing before me.

Lucy rushes up to us, and I hug her.

"Look," Caro says. She points to the sky.

Clouds are darkening the entire bowl of the sky, moving quickly, as if a horrible storm is coming.

"She's here," Lucy whispers.

Motherbird runs to us. "Andria is here," she says. She looks at Lucy, and she looks at Caro. Then she says, "Your mother has returned."

Lucy stares at Caro. "Your mother?" Lucy says.

"Our mother," Caro says. "Yes."

Lucy takes a deep breath, and then nods. "Of course," she says. A smile crosses her face, and she says, "I've always wanted a sister."

"I know where we can go," Caro tells us. "Hurry up."

The sky continues to darken. "Fall back!" we hear. It is Jonn's voice. "Fall back!"

Beth & Kay

Kay Fraser and Beth Bracken are a designer-editor team in Minnesota.

Kay is from Buenos Aires. She left home at eighteen and moved to North Dakota—basically the exact opposite of Argentina. These days, she designs books, writes, makes tea for her husband, and drives their daughters to their dance lessons.

Beth and her husband live in a light-filled house with their son, Sam, and their daughter, Etta. Beth spends her time editing, reading, daydreaming, and rearranging her furniture.

Kay and Beth both love dark chocolate, Buffy, and tea.

Odessa

Odessa Sawyer is an illustrator from Santa Fe, New Mexico. She works mainly in digital mixed media, utilizing digital painting, photography, and traditional pen and ink.

Odessa's work has graced the book covers of many top publishing houses, and she has also done work for various film and television projects, posters, and album covers.

Highly influenced by fantasy, fairy tales, fashion, and classic horror, Odessa's work celebrates a whimsical, dreamy, and vibrant quality.